AF512338

They Dare To Enjoy

They Dare To Enjoy

Air Marshal **AV Vaidya** PVSM, VM (Retd)

KNOWLEDGE WORLD

KW Publishers Pvt Ltd
New Delhi

KNOWLEDGE WORLD
KW Publishers Pvt Ltd
NEW DELHI: 4676/21, First Floor, Ansari Road, Daryaganj, New Delhi 110002
E mail@kwpub.in/knowledgeworld@vsnl.net T +91.11.23263498 / 43528107
MUMBAI: 15 Jay Kay Industrial Estate, Linking Road Extn., Santacruz (W), Mumbai 400054
E mumbai@kwpub.in T +91.22.26614110 / 26613505

www.kwpub.in

All rights reserved. No part of this book may be reproduced or transmitted in any form or by any means, electronic or mechanical, including photocopying, recording or by any information storage and retrieval system, without permission in writing.

ISBN 10: 81-87966-86-6
ISBN 13: 978-81-87966-86-9

© 2009, Air Marshal AV Vaidya

Published by Kalpana Shukla, KW Publishers Pvt Ltd
4676/21, First Floor, Ansari Road, Daryaganj, New Delhi 110002

Printed at Sapra Brothers New Delhi

Contents

Preface		vii
1.	Vikram Learns the Secret of Joy	1
2.	Birth and Growth of Defence Aviation	3
3.	Functioning of an Air Force Station	9
4.	A Glance into the Cockpit	15
5.	Unmanned Aerial Vehicle	21
6.	The Longest Day	27
7.	Flight Safety Meetings	31
8.	Air Defence	35
9.	Shooting Down of F-104 in 1971 War	47
10.	Ground Attack Weapons	51
11.	Gunnery Meet	59
12.	War Gaming	65
13.	Night Flying	71
14	The Dare Devils	79

Preface

This is not a story. This is merely a compilation of various activities in the life of a fighter pilot and his colleagues. It is a collection of his and his friends' experiences during their glorious service put in by them in the Indian Air Force (IAF) as fighter pilots. The aim of this narration, similar to the aim I had set while writing the earlier book "Wings of Joy", is to acquaint the young generation and their parents about the functioning of an Air Force (not necessarily the Indian Air Force) and, particularly, about fighter flying. It is really unfortunate that many of us are unaware of what joys and thrills this profession has to offer. I hope this book will achieve its aim and open the doors wider for youngsters to become fighter pilots and "**dare to enjoy**" a very challenging profession.

1 ▸ Vikram Learns the Secret of Joy

As a young boy, Vikram used to enjoy performing challenging things. He loved performing that task where there was danger involved, as he got addicted to the immense joy that he experienced after accomplishing it successfully. He learnt this secret of joy when he was just about eight years old. Surprisingly, the secret was revealed to him by a small culvert that was next to his house. The culvert was dirty and normally, people didn't take a chance of jumping over it. They walked a little distance and took the small bridge. To Vikram, this meant some extra unnecessary to and fro walking and waste of precious ten minutes, which he thought could be utilised in lazing in the bed.

His school was on the other side and he had to negotiate this culvert practically every day. So one day after gathering a lot of courage, he dared to jump across but just missed reaching the other side and fell in the dirty waters. Luckily he wasn't hurt but his clothes were all messed up and he had to go back home to change them. Some people who saw him fall laughed, some elders scolded him but nobody really came forward with the intention of helping him. Nobody inspired him by saying, "Doesn't matter young man. Try again. One day you will succeed and use the saved time for doing more studies. But practice jumping elsewhere first and once your long jump exceeds the breadth of the culvert, then leap across it". When he reached home, his mother also scolded him and warned him not to do such a thing again.

But Vikram was not the kind who would give up so easily. He seriously took to broad jumping and after achieving adequate confidence, he decided to jump across the culvert one day and he made it. The joy of having finally achieved the goal was intoxicating. Thereafter, he continued to persevere in jumping longer and longer, participated in the school athletics competition and won it by setting higher and higher standards for himself. Vikram had found the answer to make life interesting. He was surprised that the answer was so simple —"Just challenge oneself to do things. Achieve them and feel happy. But keep the high jump bar at achievable yet challenging height, or else one may break one's leg."

2 ▸ Birth and Growth of Defence Aviation

Wing Commander (Wg Cdr) Ajai Shukla was a fighter pilot, who was currently posted in the locally based fighter squadron. As a part of Indian Air Force (IAF) enrollment scheme to motivate young boys to join the IAF, some pilots were in turn, requested to visit the nearby schools and give a lecture to the school children to make them aware of the various aspects of this profession. School children were also invited to the nearby Air Force bases and shown the functioning of the base, including active flying. On a Saturday, Wg Cdr Shukla was requested to visit Vikram's school and deliver a lecture. Vikram was eagerly waiting to see what this fighter pilot looked like and to hear what he had to say. When Vikram saw this trim, handsome, smart looking officer in his immaculate uniform, with the flying wing prominently displayed on the left side of his chest, he was really impressed. When Shukla commenced his speech, all the children, including Vikram were almost mesmerised.

Shukla started by telling all the attentive students how aviation came into being, how the potential that lay in the third dimension, that is the vertical dimension mainly of air was realised and how technology developed at a very rapid rate towards the exploitation of this third dimension. His talk covered the birth and growth of defence-related-aviation and went something like what follows.

It is often forgotten that the Air Force is comparatively a very young Service and is yet to complete even a century. In fact, one of the first Air Forces, the Royal Air Force (RAF) was created in 1918. The Army is perhaps as old as mankind and came into being ever since man started fighting on the ground in an organised manner. The Navy too is hundreds of years old and dates back to around 16th century, when economic interests clashed over the sea and battles were fought between ships to establish dominance over blue waters. But young as it may be, the pace of advance in the field of aviation has been phenomenal, because of the realisation of the tremendous potential available in the use of the third dimension. This realisation set about a fierce race amongst the leading nations for outsmarting and surprising the enemy with technological innovations.

Aviation began soon after the successful flight made by the Wright brothers in 1904. Subsequently, it gave birth to a term called "air power" which meant the ability of a nation to cause damage to the enemy through the medium of air. In the early decades of the century, the term air power basically included aircraft alone, because nothing else other than aircraft used the medium of air. As time passed, science and technology brought in a vast array of other users such as missiles, satellites, various types of weapons and the definition of air power had to be accordingly modified time and again.

With the induction of satellites, ballistic missiles and weaponisation of space in the near future, the term "air power" is being replaced by a more encompassing word namely "aerospace power", the widely accepted working definition of which is, "The ability of a nation to project military force by or from a platform in the third dimension above the surface of the earth." The third dimension includes outer space and the use of word Air Power is now deemed to encompass the exploitation of space as well.

The first use of this third dimension was made years back in the form of balloons which were used as observation posts. The Army

Commander was always very inquisitive to know what is happening on the other side of the battlefront. This curiosity was well-satisfied by an observer, hoisted at around 100 to 200 ft above the ground in a balloon, who provided adequate intelligence (information about the deployment of enemy forces) to the Army Commander to formulate a winning plan. But such a scheme had limitations in terms of visibility, mobility, weather and depth of reconnaissance (reccee). To some extent, these limitations were overcome towards the end of the first decade of the 20th century, when heavier than air machines (meaning aircraft) took to the air and could stay airborne for a reasonable length of time.

The first use that an aircraft was put to was that of reccee and observation. The pilot often crossed over the battle lines, flew without any worries into the enemy's airspace, looked down, studied the enemy's dispositions and narrated what he had seen to the Army Commander, who finally took the credit for winning that battle.

Very soon, the enemy too got hold of similar machines and nullified the advantage. The opposing pilots often crossed each other in the air, with friendly waves and salutes born through professional camaraderie, till one day, one of them pulled out a pistol and started shooting at the other. Thus, began the battle for dominance of the air, also called in military terms as "battle for air superiority", which was to see only escalation and no end in time to come. The aim of shooting at the other pilot was to gain back the advantage which was lost as a result of the other side also acquiring aerial capability. Very simply, the aim was to deny the enemy the use of the air, while ensuring its use for own interests.

This use of the air which initially started with reccee and observation soon attained an offensive nature, whereby ammunition was carried on board these aircraft and dropped on the enemy deployed on the flanks and in depth. Mountains, rivers, forests and other natural obstructions which gave an excellent cover to the ground forces from enemy's ground fire soon appeared to lose their value. This tremendously important revelation and introduction to the vast domain of the potential of air power soon plunged all leading countries into a rat race for devising newer and better ways and means of denying the enemy the use of air, while retaining its use for themselves.

Initially, when air power came into being, there were basically two schools of thought about the methodology of its use in warfare. One school of thought, mainly backed by the Germans, Russians and Japanese during World War II firmly believed that air power must get subjugated to the ground power and that its best usage lay in giving total support to the ground forces in the Tactical Battle Area (TBA), which is the area on either side of the border in which the opposing ground forces were fighting. The leadership then strongly felt that Air Power was restricted to support the fast moving ground troops and that it did not have an independent mission of its own. The German concept of *blitzkrieg* is a classic example which enunciated a combined and well-integrated thrust with tank power, air power and man power, all put together to bear on the enemy at sensitive places and it was believed and amply proven that no opposition could halt such a massive and well-coordinated thrust. This school of thought felt that air power had very little application beyond the TBA.

The other school of thought held by the Americans, British and Italians felt that air power had much wider use than merely its application in the TBA. They felt that subjugating air power to the Army and restricting its use to the TBA alone amounted to gross under utilisation of air power. They felt that air power had an independent identity like ground power or sea power and that with its inherent flexibility and manoeuvrability, it could be used far more effectively in strategic form, meaning by attacking enemy's targets located well beyond the TBA in her heartland. They used their air power to destroy and dislocate the German military, industrial and economic system, with the aim of undermining the morale of the German people to the point, where their capacity for armed resistance is fatally weakened.

The differences in the ideologies regarding the use of air power between the two sides that fought World War II were quite obvious from the way their air power was utilised. Air power with its application in various forms during World War II and with differing doctrines finally proved its independent identity and potential and very soon, it was generally accepted that the strategic role of air power was as important, if not more, than its tactical usage in direct support of the Army.

As is evident today from the last few wars fought in Kosovo, Iraq and Afghanistan, the strategic role of air power has come to stay and air power will perhaps be used increasingly in strategic role rather than in tactical role.

Wg Cdr Shukla spoke for over an hour leaving all the students spellbound. He ended his talk after telling them about some of the latest aircraft which he had flown and which were challenging and, hence, pleasurable to fly. The children gave him a standing applause and requested him to come again and tell them something more about his thrilling experiences during his illustrious career as a fighter pilot. Wg Cdr Shukla invited the children to the Air Force base and promised to show them the entire functioning of the base, including flying. The students cheered in excitement and readily accepted the invitation.

3 ▸ Functioning of an Air Force Station

A month later, Wg Cdr Shukla, after taking the permission of his Boss, spoke to the Principal of the school which he had visited and requested him to send the interested students to the Air Force station on the following Saturday. The Principal agreed readily and asked Shukla whether he too could come along. Shukla was quite amused by the interest shown by the Principal.

Following Saturday, the children arrived as planned and they were taken straight to the Briefing Room where the meteorological briefing (Met Briefing) was being held. Though called a Met Briefing, it actually covered all aspects related to the flying activities that day. The weatherman customarily was the first person to brief. After studying various Isothermal (lines joining places having same temperature), Isobaric (lines joining places having same pressure) charts, wind speeds at various heights, latest satellite pictures, etc, he gave his prediction of what kind of weather to expect.

That particular day, he had predicted clear skies till around 1400 hrs. Thereafter, he expected some low clouds (about four octas), coming from over the sea on the west. Vikram wanted to know what octas meant. Shukla explained to him that an octa is a unit of measuring the quantity of clouds in the sky. If the sky is fully covered, then the cloud amount is said to be eight octas. If half the sky is covered, the cloud amount is said to be four octas. The Met Officer warned the pilots that visibility may reduce considerably and they may need to resort to instrument aided approach for landing and that all those who are scheduled to land after 1200 hrs should exercise adequate caution. He did not expect any rain.

Shukla told the students that the appearance of low clouds (as low as 200-300 ft from the ground level) can be very disturbing. These clouds can hide the runway (R/W) and make it invisible even when the pilot is very close to the runway during his approach for landing. This is the time when he needs to make use of the Instrument Landing System (ILS) or the Ground Controlled Approach (GCA). He said more about this later.

The next man to come and brief was the Air Traffic Control (ATC) Officer called the Duty Air Traffic Control Officer (DATCO). In short, the prime responsibility of a DATCO is to control the air traffic so that all the take-offs and landings are well-regulated. He reported that the runway was fully serviceable, meaning that it had been inspected and found fit for operations.

The DATCO also briefed about the serviceability of various flying related equipments like ILS, GCA, AD 210, NDB, TACAN, etc not only at that airbase, but at neighbouring airbases as well. The students were confused. They wanted to know what these terms meant. Shukla explained to them that when a pilot takes off and goes away from the airfield, he, at times, needs guidance to come back, particularly in bad weather like rain, poor visibility, low clouds, etc. There are two types of systems available to help him. There are specially designed systems to help him approach the airfield called as "Airfield Approach Systems" which bring him towards the airfield and there are systems to help him execute a safe landing called the "Runway Approach Systems". AD 210, popularly called as a Homer, is a system which tells a pilot which magnetic course to steer to arrive over the airfield. When a pilot talks to the DATCO on his wireless communication system, AD 210 equipment immediately points towards the direction from which the pilot's radio transmission has come. The DATCO then simply tells that pilot to steer that course to arrive home. The Non Directional Beacon (NDB) and Tactical Air Navigation (TACAN) are systems which also do the same job. These systems transmit signals which the on board aircraft system analyses and presents on the circular dial in the cockpit, the direction which the pilot should steer to reach the airfield. There are some systems which also tell the pilot through a digital display the distance of his aircraft from the selected airfield.

Even after coming overhead the airfield, there are times when the runway is not visible to the pilot. This is a situation when he needs what are called as the runway approach systems. Such situations are quite common, particularly in rainy season when there are plenty of clouds, fog and mist during winters and dust haze during summers. In such conditions, systems like the Instrument Landing System (ILS) and Ground Controlled Approach (GCA) come to the rescue of the pilot. Both these systems are capable of keeping three dimensional tracks (elevation, azimuth and distance) of the aircraft in relation to the landing runway. With the help of display instruments in the cockpit, the ILS system guides the pilot to arrive at the touchdown point. It is a pilot interpreted system. The GCA makes use of radars called the Surveillance Radar (SRE) and Precision Approach Radar (PAR) and referring to the display on the radar screens, the GCA controller guides the pilot to arrive safely at the touchdown point. The GCA controllers are very qualified people with lot of experience. Children seemed satisfied, though not entirely.

Then, it was the Engineering Officer's turn to give the briefing. He told about the serviceability of aircraft available that day to fly. The state and watch hours of various radars deployed at base and nearby in the local flying area was also covered. Shukla explained to the students that these radars were required to give surveillance to the aircraft flying around the airfield. In other words, the controllers watching the scope of these radars generally kept track of who is where, ensured that no aircraft strays away from its designated area, thus ensuring that no collision takes place between the various aircraft present in the air. They also assist the pilot to reach the airfield when he wants to go back for landing. They are also used extensively to train pilots in carrying out successful interception missions. These missions are carried out to intercept and shoot down enemy aircraft if they violate the international border either in peace, or during war. Students wanted to know how the interceptions are carried out to which Shukla replied that he will take them to the radar operational room and explain the entire activity there. Hearing him, the students were overjoyed.

Shukla then took the children to the Air Traffic Control Tower from where they could watch the entire runway and fighter aircraft taking off and landing. All the students were extremely excited and wanted Shukla uncle to visit their school again and tell them more about the various exciting experiences in the activity of fighter flying. Shukla promised to do so. The Head Master was also highly impressed and told Shukla that he was welcome anytime he wished to visit the school.

A Typical Air Traffic Control Tower

A Modern Cabin in an ATC

4 ▸ A Glance into the Cockpit

Vikram and one of his friends named Inder were highly impressed by what had been told to them about the Air Force so far. They wanted to know more and so they caught hold of Wg Cdr Shukla after the talk and pleaded, "Uncle, can we visit the airbase again and will you please show us the cockpit?" Shukla was impressed by the honest interest shown by these two and invited them a week later to show the cockpit. He even promised to let them sit in the cockpit and see the various instruments, taking help of which the pilot flies his fighter aircraft. Both of them were overjoyed and eagerly waited for these seven days to be over.

A week later, when Vikram and Inder came to the airbase, Shukla first took them to his squadron and showed them a picture of how a cockpit of an aircraft looked during the period of World War II. He told them in brief about the various basic instruments that were there in the cockpit and how those brave pilots flew their fighters with very basic information available to them.

He told them that the cockpit in those days had very few instruments like the Air Speed Indicator (ASI), the altitude indicator called the Altimeter, Verticle Speed Indicator (VSI) which indicated the rate at which the aircraft was climbing or descending, magnetic compass to tell the pilot which direction the aircraft was going, Turn and Slip Indicator (TSI) to indicate which side and with what rate the aircraft was turning, Artificial Horizon (A/H) and few engine instruments. Have a look at some of the typical cockpits of World War II.

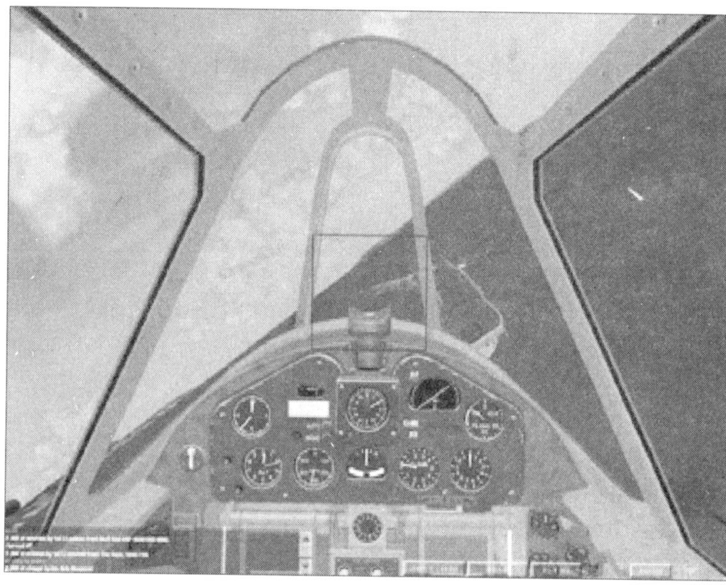

Typical Cockpit of an Aircraft of World War II

Another Instrument Panel of a World War II Aircraft

This is a picture of an Altimeter which indicates to the pilot the height of the aircraft. The small needle indicates in thousands while the big needle indicates in hundreds. If the small needle is between 4 and 5 and the big needle is on 7, it means the aircraft is at 4,700 ft above mean sea level (AMSL). Presently, it indicates that the aircraft is on the ground at sea level.

Altimeter

The picture below is of a Verticle Speed Indicator (VSI). When an aircraft is climbing, it indicates to the pilot at what rate it is climbing. If the needle is on .5, it means the aircraft is climbing at 500 feet per minute, or in other words it will take one full minute to climb 500 feet. Similarly, if the needle is on 1.5, it means the aircraft is climbing at the rate of 1,500 feet per minute. If it is below zero, it means the aircraft is descending. And if the needle is on zero, it means the aircraft is neither climbing nor descending – it is going level.

Vertical Speed Indicator

Next, have a look at the primitive Air Speed Indicator (ASI). This instrument indicates to the pilot the speed of the aircraft at which he is flying. Presently, the instrument indicates that the aircraft is flying at 170

Air Speed Indicator

Kilometre per hour (Kmph). Aircraft speed is generally measured in either Kmph or nautical miles (Kts) per hour.

What I have shown you so far are pictures of some primitive instruments. Now, have a look at the picture below. This is a picture of what is called as the Head Up Display (HUD). Modern aircraft of today have done away with analogue instruments because they are more prone to errors and at times, difficult to comprehend. Modern aircraft now use computers and have switched over to digital presentation of instruments. The picture below shows a very basic display giving the speed, height, rate of descent,etc which is projected to the pilot on his front wind screen at his eye level. Thus, the pilot does not have to look in the cockpit to get this information.

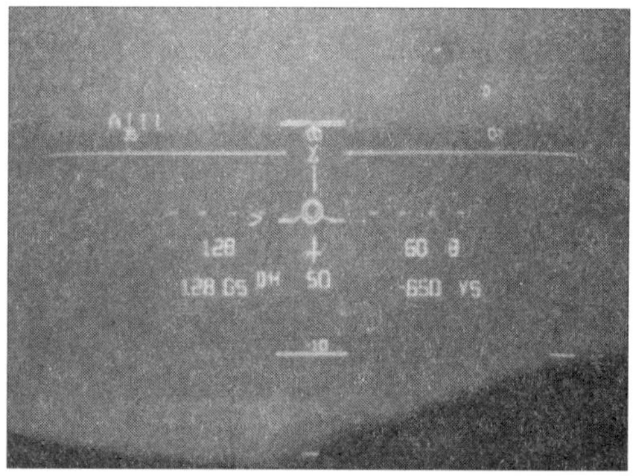

A Basic Head Up Display

Shown below are the pictures of two cockpits. The first one is MiG-23 aircraft which is not very modern and the other is F-18 aircraft which is state-of-the-art, meaning most modern. The MiG-23 aircraft, in fact, does not have any modern instrumentation and you can see plethora of instruments and switches which a single pilot has to handle. As against that, you can see the F-18 cockpit which looks so neat and pilot-friendly. By and large, the Russian aircraft starting from the MiG-15 series to Mig-29 had analogue

MiG-23 Cockpit

F-18 Cockpit

display instruments. It's only a few years back that the Russians have also switched to digital display instrumentation.

Sample Displays on two MFDs

The latest trend is to use MFDs (Multi-Function Displays). These MFDs can be used to display various information like instruments, maps, weapon aiming indices, etc and are very easy to comprehend.

Thereafter, Wg Cdr Shukla took both the boys to the aircraft and made them sit one by one in the cockpit. Both Vikram and Inder were so fascinated that they decided to become fighter pilots. They wanted to know more about the thrilling experiences that Shukla and his other pilot friends had experienced. Shukla promised to do so.

5 ▶ Unmanned Aerial Vehicle

A month later, Wg Cdr Shukla rang up the Principal and informed him that he would like to visit the school on coming Saturday. He sensed the excitement in the Principal's voice when he told him, "Of course Wing Commander, you are always welcome."

Shukla carried some photographs of the unmanned aerial vehicle (UAV) and also the photographs taken by the sensors carried on board by the UAV. He also took along with him Wg Cdr Ashok Mehta who was the Commanding Officer (CO) of the locally based UAV squadron. As they entered the auditorium, the children stood up and gave them a warm welcome by clapping their hands. Shukla began his talk as follows: "Good morning friends, this morning I have brought along with me Wg Cdr Ashok Mehta who will tell you about the unmanned aerial vehicles called UAVs for short. They are also called as Pilotless Vehicles by some. But first, let me tell you about the basic functions which any Air Force in the world has to perform. There is nothing secret about these functions.

Firstly, any Air Force must be able to guard the skies of her country, meaning that no aircraft or object that flies should be able to cross the border and enter our airspace uninformed and unnoticed and if it does, then the Air Force must have the capability to shoot it down. This activity is termed as air defence and we will talk about it in detail later. The second function is to attack the enemy targets located across the border and destroy them. This is called as ground attack capability. The third important function is to monitor what is happening across the border. This is called as reconnaissance function or intelligence gathering function. There are many other functions about which we will talk later. Wg Cdr Mehta, who is here with me today, is an expert in performing the function of reconnaissance (reccee). He is commanding the UAV squadron which you all saw the other day when you visited the air base. He will narrate to us one of his experiences which is very interesting and thrilling. Over to Wg Cdr Mehta."

Wg Cdr Mehta, also a trim, smart, handsome fighter pilot came to the podium and began his speech that follows like this: "Friends, I will narrate to you a live situation that I experienced a few days back. Incidentally, before that, let me tell you that all the Air Forces in this world have these UAVs and they are frequently and extensively used to enter discreetly into enemy's airspace and hunt for enemy's vital targets and photograph them. Well, my squadron primarily does this job which is indeed very interesting to perform. To be able to see the adversary's targets based on the ground and also generally camouflaged, the UAV has to carry various sensors like optical cameras which are used to photograph targets on a clear day with good visibility. They also carry infrared cameras to see the targets in bad visibility at night and even through the camouflage. Let me show you some sample pictures of the UAVs.

A UAV in take-off mode

A small UAV used by the German Army

UAV named Pioneer used by the US in the Gulf and Iraq Wars

Notice the sensors under the nose, wings and fuselage of Pioneer. There are small UAVs and there are big UAVs as well. The small ones can remain in the air for few hours, while the big ones can stay as long as, or even more than 30 hours. Some can climb only a few thousand feet while some can climb even more than 30,000 feet.

Have a look at some infrared photographs and one taken by an optical camera during day time from the air.

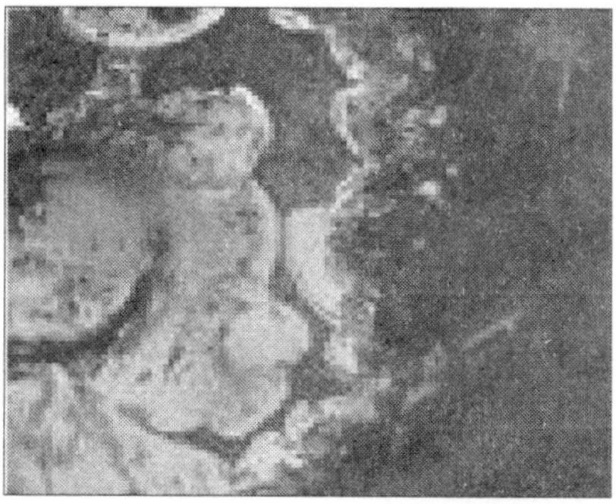

Sample IR Photograph

Another Sample IR Photograph

Sample Day Light
Normal Camera Photograph

One evening, when I was supposed to be on night duty, I got an urgent call from the operations room (Ops room) that an important information had been received from the Intelligence Department. They had intercepted an enemy message that large scale infiltration by terrorists was likely to take place in a particular sector that night. I was given the details of the place where likely infiltration was to take place and then tasked to launch two UAVs to reccee that area to locate the infiltrators.

You may first like to know how the UAV functions, how it is controlled and how it captures intelligence. Well, to put it very simply, the UAV is just like any aircraft as far as its construction goes. The only difference is the pilot instead of sitting in the UAV is actually outside on the ground. He is called as the external pilot and controls the UAV through wireless communication — just like a model aircraft is flown. Some of you might have flown these model aircraft, or at least seen them during your training in NCC, or in some exhibitions. The external pilot can make the UAV take-off, turn, navigate from one point to another, bring it back and make it land. The UAV has computers which can be pre-programmed to follow a particular route and come back home. The UAVs are primarily used because they are very difficult to detect by radars and, hence, very difficult to shoot down. Since they are unmanned, no human life is endangered.

UAV Ground Control Station

The UAVs are connected and controlled from a Ground Control Station (GCS). The computer on board the UAV is in continuous dialogue with the GCS. Whatever the cameras mounted on the UAV see, the same is transmitted in real time to the GCS TV screen. This is similar to watching a live programme like a cricket match seen by you on your home TV which is being filmed by Doordarshan. Sitting in the GCS, are the photo-interpreters, who carefully and continuously watches the screen. They can zoom in or out as desired. They can also remotely turn the camera lens to left or right and scrutinise the desired area in greater detail.

On receiving the message from the Ops room, I rushed to the squadron and gathered the required crew and technicians to launch the two UAVs. In less than an hour, as the night was setting in, both the UAVs were airborne. Our UAVs were programmed to stay in the air for a little over fifteen hours, so I was quite sure that I will be able to catch the infiltrators on my camera and get to know their location, even if the infiltration takes place in the early hours of the morning—that is almost ten hours after the UAVs were airborne. I knew it was going to be a long night for me and that my eyes will get strained. I had another observer sitting along with me. We couldn't see anything till almost two in the morning, but surprisingly even at two, we both were not sleepy or tired. Instead, we were quite charged and determined to locate the infiltrators.

Half an hour later, we suddenly noticed some unusual movement in a narrow valley. We immediately zoomed in our cameras to have a closer look and were pleasantly surprised to find that some human beings were approaching the border. They were still five-odd kilometere from the border and we estimated that the crossing might take place in about two hours. We contacted the Ops room and informed them about their position and expected time of infiltration. The officer on duty in the Ops room, in turn, contacted the Command Headquarters (Command HQ) and relayed the information that we had given them. The rest of the job was done by our Indian Army and the Border Security Force (BSF) personnel. We felt great to hear in the National TV news channel the next day, that an attempt by some terrorists had been thwarted by the Indian Army and BSF personnel and that they had managed to kill five terrorists and severely wound as many without loss of any life on our side. Well, we didn't mind the entire credit going to the jawans and felt very happy and satisfied that our hard work and perseverance had paid dividends. Thank you all very much for giving me a patient hearing. I hope you found this incidence quite exciting."

The children were thrilled. Not just the children but even the staff members, teachers and the Principal seemed to be listening totally engrossed. They were so impressed that all of them requested Wg Cdr Shukla and Wg Cdr Mehta to visit them again and tell them more about their or some other pilot's exciting experiences. Before leaving, Wg Cdr Shukla gave Vikram an article to read which is written by Wg Cdr Vaidya that tells about his live experience during the Maldives operation. He said,"Read this article. It is very interesting and will tell you how air power can be projected so quickly, so far and so effectively."

6 ▸ The Longest Day

Vikram couldn't wait to reach home and commence reading the article. He was so impressed by what he had heard and seen about flying that he wanted to know more and more about this profession. The article is quoted below in Wg Cdr Vaidya's own words.

"It was November 3, 1988, when I realised how the day's proceedings can go completely haywire and can be full of strangest of surprises. Normally, one likes to plan one's day and generally feel happy to see that events do take place as planned with minor diversions. But then, there are times when unforeseen events take precedence and one is left utterly helpless. November 3, 1988 also turned out to be the longest day in my life. On this day, I had to perform and perform well, hardly with any rest.

I was commanding a Mirage-2000 squadron which was located at Gwalior then. The Command Flight Safety meeting was organised in Command HQ at Bamrauli, Allahabad on November 3, 1988, which all the Commanding Officers (COs) and Flight Safety Officers (FSOs) were required to attend. The meeting was to start at 0900 hrs sharp. We were tasked by Command to take off from Gwalior at 0530 hrs in an Avro (transport aircraft used for transporting personnel from place to place). We were also told to pick up other COs and FSOs en route from other airfields and reach Allahabad by 0830 hrs. To achieve this task, we had to get up as early as 0430 hrs and board the aircraft before 0520 hrs. Having picked up other officers, we reached Allahabad well in time and had a hearty breakfast and a good cup of tea.

Sharp at 0900 hrs, the Air Officer Commanding-in-Chief (AOC-in-C) of that Command walked in and the proceedings started. At 1200 hrs, the conference broke up for tea, and I was told to immediately go and see the Senior Air Staff Officer (SASO) in charge of operations. He quite coolly said to me, "Vaidya, you have to take eight aircraft to Trivandrum right away. I just got a call from Air Headquarters (Air HQ) Ops Room (which is located in Delhi) and mind you these orders are straight from the Chief so don't mess up." Trivandrum! —never had I thought in my wildest dreams that I would be required to go to Trivandrum and that too in such a panic. The SASO told me that if I had any doubts, or if I wanted any more information, I could talk to the Director of Operations, who was available in the Air HQs Ops Room. When I rang him up he told me, "Vaidya, sorry to surprise you like this but please take eight aircraft quickly to Trivandrum. There is some foul up in Male. The Maldives State Government is under threat from guerillas and we need you to go there quickly."

Here, I was in Allahabad, so far away from my squadron and it was past midday— how am I going to take eight aircraft to Trivandrum and that too that very day! Well, I immediately got in touch with my Flight Commander (Flt Cdr) (Senior most officer working under me) in Gwalior and told him, "Stop flying. Get all aircraft in three tank configuration. Prepare maps for Trivandrum and as the aircraft get ready, start taking off in pairs for Trivandrum. I shall join you shortly." He nearly dropped the receiver when he heard this. "Sir, are you sure we are required to go to Trivandrum?" He, too, apparently had never dreamt that he will be asked to go to Trivandrum of all places and that too in such a hurry. I had to shake him out of his dazed state, so I said, "Yes Trivandrum and I repeat Trivandrum and I haven't gone crazy as yet. And don't tell at home that we are going to Trivandrum. Instruct everyone that no one is to disclose our destination. This mission is to be treated as highly classified—strictly need to know basis— do you understand? —so are the orders," I said.

So the Flt Cdr got on with the job. He told the Squadron Technical Officer (STO) who was also stunned for a while. So were the squadron pilots, who had least expected such an order, but they started the preparations in real earnest. I got myself an Avro aircraft to drop me immediately from Allahabad to Gwalior and reached Gwalior by about 1630 hrs and I found my Flt Cdr about to proceed to the first pair of fighters, which had been made ready. I wished him luck and told him that I would follow him in the next pair of aircraft which I was told would be ready in 45 minutes or so. I rushed home, packed some items in a hurry and was back in less than 30 minutes.

I was told that the next pair of aircraft would be ready in fifteen minutes. I quickly briefed the other fighter pilot (called as No 2) who was to follow me in another aircraft. The flying time was a little over 2 hrs 30 min and I estimated that we would be landing at Trivandrum at around 2000 hrs. This meant that part of our journey would be at night and in dark phase and so also the landing and that too at a totally unknown airfield.

We finally took off at around 1730 hrs, climbed to as high as 40,000 ft, engaged autopilot and kept chugging along. Sitting strapped up in a fighter cockpit in care of autopilot for so long and with nothing worthwhile to do is not an easy task. We had to spend nearly two-and-a-half hours in that state but somehow time passed. Bhopal, Nagpur, some passing airliners, certain amount of radar work on them, beautiful sunset, Banglore, whole lot of clouds (thanks to Northeast monsoons) and frequent lightening made the ferry quite interesting. It is amazing to see how lightening can fill up the entire sky in dark night, making one wonder whether to go up, down, left or right to avoid them. I had told my No 2 to keep me in radar contact and keep trailing by two kilometre which he did. We finally reached and executed a safe landing in slight drizzling. We were really grateful to God for not having given us any emergency.

Safe landing at Trivandrum was not the end of that day's story. I was soon summoned by the AOC-in-C who had set up his office in a tent pitched on the tarmac next to the runway. He briefed me on the Male crisis and asked me to stand-by with six aircraft to take off next day at 0600 hrs with loaded guns. The gun ammunition was expected to arrive by 2300 hrs in another transport aircraft. After receiving the ammo and leaving the loading operations to the STO, we pilots packed up around midnight since we had to fly early morning the next day.

The next day we were back at 0530 hrs. The AOC-in-C ordered four aircraft to demonstrate our airpower over Male islands. We decided to go in 2s and I took off along with my No 2 around 0700 hrs and headed towards Male which is almost 600 km from the coast. Flying over the sea in a single engine aircraft was an experience by itself. Male is a beautiful cluster of many islands and since I was ordered to demonstrate our Air power, I along with my No 2 flew very low over all those islands to show the locals that our Air Power was with them and to protect them. We could see the locals waving at us and clapping. Thereafter, we returned and as told by the AOC-in-C, we also demonstrated to the people of Trivandrum what fighters looked like since they had probably never seen fighters before. It was indeed a memorable mission."

Vikram enjoyed reading the article. He was amazed to read how the squadron had responded so promptly and so meticulously and at such a short notice. He was convinced of the flexibility and speed at which Air Power operates and about which so much had been told to him by Wg Cdr Shukla. Vikram had one doubt about the flight safety meeting so he went to meet Wg Cdr Shukla to seek a clarification. He said to him, "Uncle the article says that Wg Cdr Vaidya had gone to Command HQ for a flight safeety meeting—what is this meeting and what do they do in it?

7 ▸ Flight Safety Meetings

This is what Wg Cdr Shukla had to say, "Listen Vikram and please listen very carefully. People think that flying is a very dangerous profession. They think so because they are ill-informed about the facts. In fact, flying is a very safe profession, even fighter flying. If you ask me, driving on the roads of metropolitan cities like Delhi, Mumbai, etc is more dangerous. Flying is really safe and these flight safety meetings are held to discuss and ponder over how to make flying safer.

These flight safety meetings are held at various levels. The lowest level is the fighter squadron in which active flying is done. Once a month, all personnel of the squadron assemble and discuss threadbare those areas which they feel are weak and accident prone. The CO of the squadron chairs the meeting and then forwards the relevant points to Command HQ. Points come from other squadrons as well and the important ones are forwarded to Air HQs by all Command HQ. The Command HQ hold these meetings every six months. These points are discussed further at Air HQ and relevant instructions are then given to all squadron pilots to follow. The ultimate aim, like I said, is to make flying safer. Wg Cdr Vaidya had gone to Central Air Command (CAC) to attend the six-monthly flight safety meeting being chaired by the AOC-in-C.

It is good that you have asked me this question. Unfortunately, the general public is ill-informed about the facts and figures of the accidents that take place in the Air Force and this results in developing wrong impression about flight safety in the Air Force. And the main culprit for giving all kind of wrong information in my opinion is the media. You must have heard about the terrible publicity given by the media, newspapers and TV channels to the MiG-21 accidents. It was really ridiculous and totally misleading.

I wonder if you have watched this programme called "Akbar ka Durbar" on Star TV which aired the discussion on the subject of MiG-21 accidents. On the one side was a bereaved mother who had lost her son in a MiG-21 accident and on the other side was an Air Commodore in uniform and a retired Air Marshall. M J Akbar was the moderator / mediator. The very sight was immensely saddening for me because I could never imagine that there will come a day when the world's most popular aircraft will get publicly flogged in such a manner.

The entire so-called discussion appeared to be more of a bout between loudly and forcefully voiced sentiments by the bereaved mother versus moderately and patiently put across facts by the Air Force officers. The mother who had lost her son was trying to convey that MiG-21 is an old aircraft and no more safe to fly and should be grounded and discarded. The officers were trying to give statistics to prove that the accident rate of the MiG-21s was not as alarming as she perceived. Expression of sentiments seemed to overwhelm and she refused to understand or even listen to the logical explanations given. The general public is perhaps not quite aware of the damaging effect that such programmes as well as the various adverse articles and cartoons about the Mig-21 can cause to the morale and motivation of our young pilots. You might have also heard about some anti-MiG-21 associations formed by the afflicted with the aim of publicly declaring the Mig-21 as a flying coffin. In my honest opinion, I considered them as anti-national organisations that are extremely harmful to the security of our nation.

In my young days, *Vampire* started getting called as a flying coffin and then came the turn of the *Gnat*. We, as young pilots, always knew that such talk was all rubbish. I was flying the *Gnats* then. I think the entire MiG-21 controversy also ought to be brushed aside as nothing but absolute humbug.

The first fatal loss which I experienced in the MiG-21 was that of my coursemate who died while learning air combat. I remember meeting his mother. She was shocked and shattered but never did she ever accuse the IAF or the MiG-21 of having killed her son. She was indeed brave and prepared to accept the loss without any misplaced malice.

When I used to meet some or for that matter almost all the misinformed and ill-informed relatives and civilian friends, they sheepishly used to ask me about the reliability of the MiG-21, hoping to get the correct answer from the horse's mouth. I was not really surprised. They felt sheepish while asking this question because they felt that I was the accused party. I was really tired of telling them that please don't go by numbers. If more than half the fleet of IAF is MiG-21s, then quite naturally more than half the accidents are likely to be those of MiG-21s. The mere numbers appear big but the rate is not at all disproportionately bigger. In fact, it is lesser than some other types of aircraft. Nor is the accident rate of the IAF abnormally higher than the accident rate of any of the world's Air forces. In fact, in most cases it is less. "Then, why all this fuss?" they asked. Well, ask the media why it is sensationalising an issue, which is in fact not an issue —I used to tell them. The media does not realise what damage is being caused to the morale of our fighter pilots. Similarly, bereaved relations crying hoarse without quite knowing the facts and demeaning and defaming the MiG-21 are perhaps innocently unaware of the harm they are causing to the IAF."

Well, I hope you are convinced of what I have just told you. Flight safety is a very important subject and no efforts are spared to ensure that accident rate is reduced and kept under control. Vikram thanked Wg Cdr Shukla and reminded him that many students will be eagerly waiting on coming Saturday in school auditorium to listen about air defence and how the F-104 of Pakistan Air Force was shot down in the 71 War.

8 ▶ Air Defence

During the next visit to school, Wg Cdr Shukla took along with him a fighter pilot named Wg Cdr Menon, who had actually witnessed the shooting down of the Pakistani F-104, which came to attack the air base at Jamnagar during the 71 War. He asked Menon to tell the students about how conventional air defence is carried out by any Air Force. Shukla gave the introductory talk saying, "Respected Principal, teachers and friends, thank you all very much for giving us this opportunity to talk to you about our glorious Service. We are really impressed and feel very happy to see the interest and excitement shown by you all. Today, we have with us Wg Cdr Menon who is an expert and will talk about the activities involved in Air Defence. He will also tell you how the F-104 was shot down by a MiG-21 in Jamnagar during the 71 War. He was a young newly commissioned officer then and was lucky enough to get to witness the entire incidence. Over to Wg Cdr Menon."

Menon commenced his talk saying, "Good morning friends, I shall now explain to you how classic air defence is carried out by any Air Force. The principle of air defence is universally the same and there is nothing secret about it. All Air Forces have one of the functions in common, ie. protection of their skies, meaning that no object which flies should be able to enter their airspace without their permission and go unnoticed. To achieve this, they need to carry out surveillance of their airspace with the help of radars.

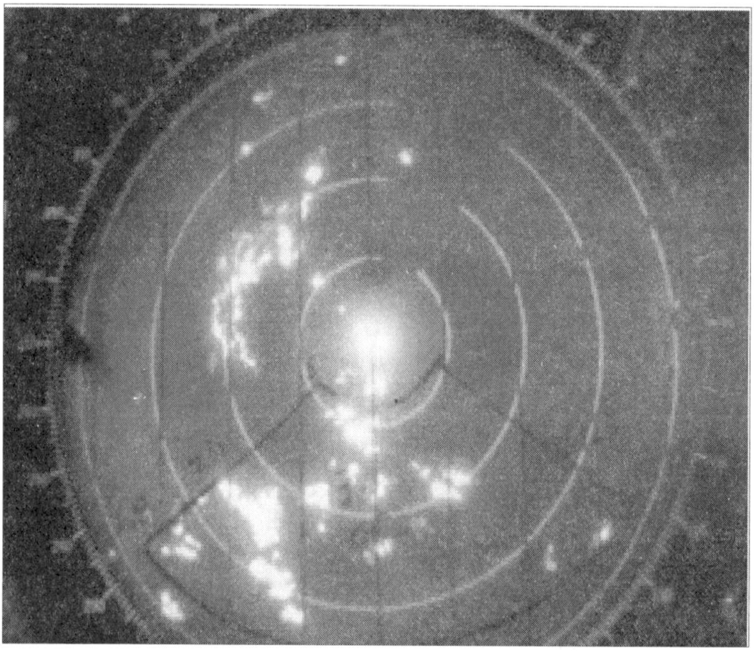

Picture of a Typical Display Screen of a Radar

A radar is a device which transmits energy in the form of electromagnetic waves and when these waves hit the surface of the aircraft flying in that area, they are reflected back by the metal used for constructing the aircraft. These reflected waves are then picked up by the same radar and are displayed on the radar screen, giving the relative position of the aircraft from the radar. Knowing the speed at which the waves travel, the distance at which the aircraft is flying is calculated by the time taken by the waves to reach the aircraft and come back. A basic radar will display in raw form even the reflections received from high grounds. This is called as noise which makes it impossible to discern the target. The ground reflections, therefore, need to be filtered out by special techniques. Modern radars resort to digital display which gives a very clean picture.

A Three Dimensional High Powered Radar

This is a picture of a High Powered Radar (HPR). Notice the huge rectangular antenna. This antenna rotates and transmits energy in all directions, thus enabling surveillance in 360 degrees around its position. If you want to spot an aircraft flying at a far distance, one needs to use lot of electrical power and pump in very strong waves which can reach far distances. A HPR is generally designed to pick up targets, flying as far as 400 to 500 km and as high as 50,000 ft. Well, what I have just told you in simple words is a very basic explanation of how a radar functions. Actually, it is quite a complicated process.

To carry out surveillance of the entire airspace round the clock of our country, you can well imagine the large number of radars that will be required. Problems get complicated because electromagnetic waves travel in straight lines. HPRs, therefore, cannot carry out effective surveillance over a large area at low levels. Specially designed low-looking radars are required to detect targets flying near the ground levels. These are generally Low Powered Radars (LPR) and can typically detect targets flying as far as 50 km or thereabouts. We also have Medium Powered Radars (MPR), which transmit waves that are powerful enough to pick up reflections from around 250 km or so. To ensure proper surveillance, one needs to create a network of radars and deploy the various radars in strategic locations. HPRs are normally static radars and once deployed in a place, they cannot be shifted. Some MPRs are movable, but not really mobile, meaning that their location can be changed but the entire process of shifting takes a few days. LPRs are classically mobile. They are mounted on vehicles and are transportable and can become operational very quickly within hours.

Below is a picture of a low looking transportable radar which is mobile and can be quickly moved from one place to another, deployed and made functional in a short time.

A Low Looking Transportable Radar

What I have told you so far is about the ground-based radars. Radar, as you may know, was invented during the World War II and deployed for the first time by the Royal Air Force (RAF) in England. It caused a revolution and tremendous damage to the Luftwaffe, the German Air Force. Since then, technology has progressed by leaps and bounds. Today, we have radars which are airborne and can see targets all around, at all levels and at great distances. Radars called Over the Horizon radars can see beyond the horizon at great distances. Below is a picture of an Aerostat. Principally, an Aerostat is a radar mounted on a balloon and taken up to around 15,000 to 20,000 ft to increase the horizon of the radar. Such a radar can see targets at all levels and as far as 300 km and above .

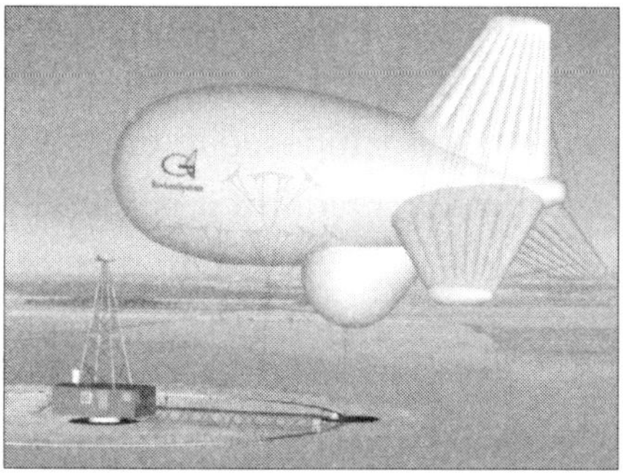

A Tethered Aerostat

E-3 Sentry

Above is the picture of Airborne Warning and Control System (AWACS). Notice the black coloured radar dome mounted piggy back. AWACS can stay airborne for 12 hrs and can give surveillance over a very large area at all levels. It also has fighter controllers on board the aircraft, who can give effective guidance to air defence aircraft for interception of targets.

While technology has produced very effective radars, many Air Forces still resort to primitive style of surveillance in the form of observation by humans as a backup arrangement, if radars fail as a result of jamming or physical destruction. MOP (Mobile Observation Post) unit classically consists of about 40 odd observers, who man around 16 observation posts, generally deployed on the border. The distance between two adjacent posts varies between five to seven kilometres, subjected to terrain. Each post is manned by two observers, who keep eyeball vigilance in turn, and report any border intrusion to the nearest operations centre. This kind of surveillance is very effective and has plugged the gap where technology has failed. They are deployed in areas where intrusions are most expected.

Air Defence basically entails four activities—Detection, Identification, Interception and Destruction. What we have seen so far is the activity of Detection. Having detected something (which is called as a track), the next important thing to do is to identify the detected track, as a friend or a foe. This is done by correlating the location of the track with the earlier obtained information about the flight path and time at which an aircraft is supposed to cross the border and enter our airspace. The incoming aircraft if it is friendly will also contact the flight controlling agency through wireless communication equipment and inform them about their entry into the airspace.

If no communication is received, the track is declared as hostile and further action of intercepting it is taken. Air Forces of all the countries maintain a certain number of aircraft armed with air-to-air weapons to shoot down hostile intruders. These aircraft are based at various air bases and are ready to take off within a short time, generally two minutes. Having taken off, they are directed by the radar controllers to intercept the intruder and shoot him down, if necessary. The picture below is that of a Light Combat Aircraft (LCA) named *Tejas* which is being developed by Hindustan Aeronautics Limited (HAL). It has its own multi-mode airborne radar, which will pick up the hostile track and the pilot will be able to shoot it down, with on board air-to-air missiles or gun.

Multi Mode Radar (MMR) on LCA

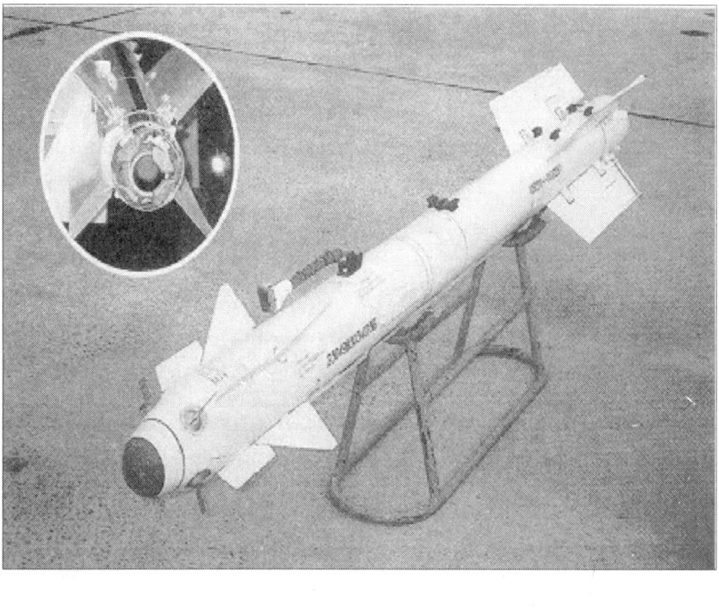

A Short Range Air-to-Air Missile

This is a picture of an air-to-air short range heat-seeking missile. This infrared heat-seeking missile when fired after it has locked onto the target follows the heat plume generated by the engine of the aircraft and collides with the aircraft destroying it. Generally, the kill range of such missiles is in the region of 4 to 8 km, depending upon the angle at which the target aircraft is being intercepted.

The picture below is that of a medium range missile. This kind of missile can have a kill range of as much as 30 to 40 km. It is guided by the aircraft radar and follows the instructions given to it by the radar till impact.

A Medium Range Air-to-Air Missile

Then, there are long range air-to-air missiles which are capable of shooting down enemy aircraft as far as over 100 km. They have an active radar in their seeker head which transmits, receives and guides the missile to its destination. These medium and long range missiles are also referred to as Beyond Visual Range (BVR) missiles.

So far, what I have described to you is the destruction of the target by firing air-to-air weapons. But if it is not possible to shoot down the enemy aircraft by intercepting it and if the hostile aircraft approach near the target which he is aiming to destroy, then ground-based air defence weapons are used to shoot him down.

A Shoulder Fired Surface-to-Air Missile

Every target which is of vital importance is always protected by surface-to-air defence weapons. The picture above is that of a Shoulder fired Missile. It is a very simple missile carried by the soldier on his shoulder, aimed at the target aircraft when seen and fired. It has a kill range of about 4 km.

A Surface-to-Air Quick Reaction Missile System

The above picture is that of a Quick Reaction Missile System. These are comprehensive systems which have their own Acquisition Radar to acquire the target aircraft, Fire Control Radars to guide the fired missile on the target. Their kill range can be as far as 20 km plus.

The last phase of air defence is provided by surface-to-air guns. These are either manual or radar controlled. Shown below is the picture of a latest missile/gun system which at any time is ready to fire 12 missiles and/or 1400 30mm rounds. The missiles are effective from 1.5 to 20 km range and from 100 to 5,000 ft height. The effective range of guns is 200 to 4,000 metres and from 100 to 4,000 feet altitude. It can fire on two targets simultaneously and has a reaction time of 4 to 6 seconds. It can also fire on the move.

A Modern Missile/Gun Air Defence System

If you recollect, I had mentioned at the beginning that any radar detects the target by transmitting electromagnetic energy and receiving back the reflected energy by the aircraft. If by some technique, the energy which strikes the aircraft is prevented from getting reflected back, then it would not be possible for the radar to detect that aircraft. This is done by what are called as stealth aircraft.

A stealth aircraft is an aircraft that uses stealth technology to make it harder to be detected by radar and other means than conventional aircraft by employing a combination of features to reduce visibility in the visual, audio, infrared and radio frequency ranges. The well-known examples include the United States' F-117 Nighthawk and the modern F-22 Raptor fighter.

F-117 Stealth Fighter of USAF

While no aircraft is totally invisible to radar, stealth aircraft limits current conventional radar's abilities to detect or track them effectively, enough to prevent an attack. Stealth is accomplished by using a complex design philosophy to reduce the ability of an opponent's sensors to detect, track and attack an aircraft. In some cases, aircraft is coated with radar absorbent paint which helps to reduce the reflected energy."

9 ▸ Shooting Down of F-104 in 1971 War

Wg Cdr Menon continued saying, "I hope you all have understood to some extent the fundamentals of air defence. Now, if I tell you how the F-104 Star Fighter of the Pakistani Air Force (PAF) was shot down in the 71 War, I am sure you will understand and enjoy better.

You may be aware that the 1971 War started on December 3, when Pakistan attacked Indian airfields in the western sector with their ground attack aircraft. India was expecting this and was quite prepared for it. The Army, Navy and Air Force were deployed in their respective operational locations ready to hit back, if Pakistan attacked. Half the fleet of aircraft of one of the Air Defence (AD) squadrons of the IAF were deployed in Jamnagar airbase, while the rest were deployed elsewhere. The squadron was then equipped with MiG-21 aircraft. The task given to the squadron located at Jamnagar was to protect the airfield and vital targets in the Saurashtra and Gujrat area. To achieve this task, the squadron had to keep its aircraft loaded with air-to-air missiles and guns ready to take-off in less than two minutes, if any border violation be reported. This activity is called as manning the ORP (Operational Readiness Platform). This operational platform is located close to the runway where these aircraft are parked inside well protected shelters. The pilots are also available close to the aircraft in underground well protected rooms. The ORP is manned round-the-clock for 24 hrs.

Jamnagar airfield had a HPR located nearby. It also had a base radar. The observation posts were also deployed all along the coast–north and west of the airfield. As a final protection, manually operated air defence guns were deployed on and around the airfield. I was told to be at the Air Traffic Control (ATC) and function as an observer. Next to me, I had a Combat Air Petrol (CAP) controller. On receiving a warning of border intrusion, the officer in Ops room ordered the aircraft on ORP to take off. These aircraft took off in less than two minutes and were either controlled by a radar that gave directions for an interception if the target aircraft was also visible on their scope or else they climbed to about 10,000 ft and orbited over the target (which is called as carrying out a CAP) waiting for the attack aircraft to arrive. Once the attack aircraft arrive and are seen by the CAP controller, he directs the CAP aircraft by giving appropriate instructions to enable them to see the attacking aircraft. This activity of manning the ORP was on for nearly three months ever since the AD squadron aircraft came to Jamnagar. The pilots and the ground crew who serviced the aircraft were getting fed up. They wanted to see action.

Then, suddenly on December 12, 1971, at 1402 hrs, the boredom was broken. One of the observation posts located on the Saurashtra sea coast reported to the Ops room in a very excited voice that two Bandits, meaning enemy aircraft were crossing the coastline and flying towards Jamnagar airfield. The officer on duty in the Ops room wasted no time and immediately ordered the aircraft on ORP to take off. Sqn Ldr BB Soni was on ORP duty at that time along with another Sqn pilot. Both of them took off without any delay and set up CAP over the airfield, waiting for the attacking aircraft. The attacking aircraft, two in number, later identified as F-104s appeared near the airfield. Their intension was to attack the aircraft parked near the runway, which, in fact, were dummies, intentionally placed in the open to deceive the attacking aircraft. The actual aircraft were hidden inside the hard protected structures called pens.

The second 104 apparently saw the MiG-21s and decided to abandon the attack and saved himself by turning away homewards towards north. The lead 104 continued to attack at high speed. This aircraft was seen by the CAP controller and he reported his position to CAP pilots. Sqn Ldr Soni happened to see him. As the F-104 finished the attack, Soni positioned himself behind him. The F-104 turned north towards Pakistan. He cleared the land and entered the sea and started flying very low and at very high speed to save himself. Soni chased him. He also descended to about 100 ft and flew at about 1,200 kmph speed with full engine power. He fired his air-to-air heat seeking missile but the pilot of F-104 was taking evasive actions by turning randomly and firing IR (Infrared) flares to misguide the missile. These flares generate similar heat source as the exhaust of the aircraft, thus, presenting many false targets to the on-coming heat seeking missile. The missile was deceived and so Soni elected to fire the guns. He went as close as 300 metres behind the F-104 and fired 23mm high explosive gun rounds which hit the F-104 which caught fire and the pilot was seen ejecting from the aircraft. The aircraft crashed into the sea. The pilot with his parachute landed in the sea. Attempts were made to rescue him but he couldn't be located. Thank you all very much for your patient hearing and if you have any questions, I will be glad to answer them after the break."

Wg Cdr Shukla then summed up the talk by saying, "OK boys, you have just heard Wg Cdr Menon how the Air Force defends its skies from the intrusion by enemy aircraft. You have also heard a very interesting and catchy narration of how the Pakistani F-104 was shot down by our Air Force. But remember that wars are not won by "defending". They are won by "attacking". In my next talk, I will tell you about the old, semi-old and the latest generation bombs, rockets and missiles that modern technology has given to the various Air Forces of the world. Let me see if I can get hold of some nice photographs which will help you to understand these weapons better. See you all after a month. Bye till then." Both Shukla and Menon were being given a standing ovation.

10 ▸ Ground Attack Weapons

A month later, Wg Cdr Shukla was invited again by the Principal to talk to the interested children. This time, he took along with him a fighter pilot named Sqn Ldr Ranjan, who was posted to a squadron equipped with ground attack aircraft. He told Ranjan to brief the students in simple language about the mechanics of carrying out ground attack. As usual, when they entered the auditorium, both of them got a huge applause. Wg Cdr Shukla commenced his introductory talk saying, "Respected Principal, teachers and dear students. Today, I have brought along with me Sqn Ldr Ranjan, who is an ace shooter. He has mastered the art of firing bombs, rockets and guns with great accuracy. He will tell us how ground attack is carried out. But before that, let me give you a little preamble. Last time, if you remember, Wg Cdr Menon spoke to us on the subject of air defence. Air defence as you have learnt is very important to prevent damage to our vital targets by intercepting the enemy's attacking aircraft, before they hit the target. The enemy too carries out air defence to shoot down our aircraft when they enter their skies to bomb their targets. Offence and defence, the two opposing elements of air power are thus in constant competition – one trying to get an upper hand on the other. Like, technology has given modern equipments to carry out air defence, at the same time technology has also given very good equipments to carry out accurate and effective attacks on ground targets. In World War II, there were what are called as dumb weapons, which had to be correctly aimed at the target and fired. But today, we have what are called as smart weapons. They have mini computers on board and can hit the target very accurately and quite independently. Sqn Ldr Ranjan will talk about them and probably, show us some pictures. Over to Sqn Ldr Ranjan."

"Good morning children," Sqn Ldr Ranjan began, "Becoming a ground attack pilot is a very challenging and, hence, a very enjoyable profession. It is challenging because one has to cross the border, enter enemy's airspace, evade the enemy's interceptor aircraft, ensure that one is not shot down by their air-to-air missiles or guns and one remains safe from the surface-to-air defence weapons deployed on and around the target and yet, amidst all that tension, drop the bombs to hit the target accurately and at the end of it come back home safe and alive. It is extremely enjoyable, because when one achieves a bulls eye on the target, the jubilation one experiences is unparalleled and if I can say as described colloquially "out of this world". As far as the Air Forces of the world are concerned, it is the ground attack pilots who face the maximum danger because they cross the border and so to say "face the bullets". The rest generally stay on their own side of the border and, hence, are quite safe.

I will now describe to you how a classic attack is carried out on an enemy target. There is nothing secret about it. Almost all Air Forces (The Royal Air Force, The American Air Force, The Israeli Air Force and others) follow similar techniques. Let us presume that we want to attack enemy's airfield which has his ground attack aircraft positioned there to attack our targets. Our aim in carrying out this airfield attack will be to damage his runway so that his aircraft cannot take-off, destroy his ATC, his bomb dump where his weapons are stored, set fire to his fuel dump, damage his communication hub, his other vital areas so that the airfield is put out of action and his attacking potential to hit our targets is thus reduced and our vital targets will, therefore, remain safe.

To execute this task what will we require? Firstly, ofcourse we will need ground attack aircraft. Then we will need weapons to attack various targets. Each target will have to be attacked with a specific ammunition which will destroy it. For example, the runway will have to be attacked with concrete piercing bombs which will cause number of big deep craters on the runway surface, making it impossible for the enemy's aircraft to take off. We will need precision attack concrete piercing high explosive bombs to destroy his bomb dump and fuel dump. We will need fire creating bombs which will set the airfield on fire and cause havoc and confusion. We will also need anti-personnel cluster bombs which spread lethal bomblets over an area and kill the personnel working on the airfield. We will need delay fuse bombs to explode at random periods of time so that his recovery is delayed. All this ammunition will have to be loaded on various ground attack aircraft. Generally, a formation of four ground attack aircraft will carry one type of ammunition, say runway damaging bombs. The RAF used these bombs while executing low level attacks on Iraqi airbases during the first Gulf War. Similarly, four other aircraft will be armed with ammunition to damage bomb and fuel dumps. Four more aircraft will carry cluster bombs and likewise. All these aircraft put together is what is called as a ground attack package.

When this package approaches the border, what do you think will the enemy do? Vikram, can you answer that question?" Vikram stood up and said, "Yes, Sir." "The enemy will do exactly what we would have done. His observation posts will report the border intrusion to his Ops room. His AD aircraft will be scrambled to intercept our ground attack aircraft and shoot them down." Ranjan continued, "You are right, Vikram. So what should we do to ensure that our strike aircraft remain safe, reach the target and deliver their weapons? Obviously, we need to tackle his interceptors with our interceptors. We should, therefore, send our AD aircraft along with the strike package and when his interceptors approach, tackle them in air combat and try and shoot them down or at least divert them away from our strike package which can proceed to the designated target unhindered. We can use our AWACS aircraft about which you have already been told. This AWACS aircraft which can see all around will warn our AD aircraft about the enemy interceptors and give them an interception on his AD aircraft. The adversary will also perhaps use similar tactics with his ground-based and airborne radar, if he has one in the air at that time. The man with better quality aircraft, AD weapons, trained pilots and better execution of tactics will finally win.

The strike package will also take evasive action by dispersing the formations in different directions to make it more difficult for radar controllers to give interception and for interceptor aircraft to pick them up. The formations will, however, continue flying towards the target. As they approach the target, they will have to tackle the surface-to-air AD weapons about which you have already been told by Wg Cdr Menon. The question that arises is how to tackle them and reduce their kill probability. There are various techniques. Since most of these weapons are radar controlled, one technique used is to send Electronic Warfare (EW) aircraft along with the strike package. These EW aircraft send powerful electromagnetic waves and jam or blind the enemy's radar, meaning the radar can no longer differentiate the target blip from the large amount of clutter created on the radar scope, thus, making that system ineffective. Yet another way is to stay out of the kill range of these weapons and fire from a distance. Such weapons are called as stand-off weapons. These are precision guided weapons which are fired from height above the kill range height of the AD weapons or from a distance more than the kill range distance of the AD weapons. Having successfully dropped the weapons on the allotted targets in the airfield complex, the strike package then returns. On their way back, they again need to ward off the threat from the enemy interceptors which are waiting to catch them. Once again the strike package is given protection by the AD escorts and the AWACS.

Well friends, what I have just told you is how an attack is carried out on enemy's target. I have described how a classic attack would be carried out on an airfield and the various considerations that have to be taken note of. Almost all the leading Air Forces of the world plan and execute their attacks in this manner. Attacks on other targets like railway yards, major communication hubs, army targets, major oil refineries, harbours, etc are carried out in more or less similar manner. Now, I will show you some of the modern weapons used for air-to-ground attack.

Laser Guided Bomb (LGB)

This is a laser guided precision attack bomb. In front of the bomb, you can see the laser guidance sensor. In simple words, laser is a very thin, sharp, powerful beam of light which is pointed towards the target by the same aircraft or another aircraft. The reflections of this laser beam coming from the target are then picked up by the bomb and the bomb is fired which follows the reflected laser beam. The target is kept illuminated with the laser till the bomb impacts.

Air-to-Ground Missile

This is a picture of a guided missile. The working principle of this kind of missile is the same as that of the LGB. The basic difference is that a bomb has no rocket motor attached to it to propel it forwards whereas a missile has. Hence, a missile can travel greater distances and can be fired from quite a distance from the target. In other words, it has a greater stand-off range.

You might wonder as to where and how do the pilots practice air-to-ground firing and become proficient in it. Well, all Air Forces have air-to-ground ranges where mock targets are created on which firing is carried out. The ammunition that is bought and kept in storage to meet any kind of unforeseen contingency has shelf life, meaning that after a certain laid down period, the explosive and other components in that ammunition deteriorate and the ammunition is no more very reliable. However, it is fit and safe enough to be fired for practise purposes. Instead of throwing away, this ammunition is given to pilots to fire on these air-to-ground ranges to improve their firing skills.

Firing of Front Gun at Air-to-Ground Practice Range

Above is a picture of an air-to-ground range on which an aircraft is firing gun ammunition. Notice, how a target of canvas has been erected. The holes made by the bullets are counted which give the score which a particular pilot has achieved. The range also has circles marked on the ground with a white flag hoisted at the centre. Pilots aim at this flag with the aircraft aiming sight and fire rockets and bombs. To encourage marksmanship, competitions are held between various squadrons and trophies are awarded to the pilots who do well and to the winning squadron. Sqn Ldr Ranjan summed up his talk by thanking all students and promised to take them to the air-to-ground range located nearby to witness live firing." The students were thrilled.

11 ▸ Gunnery Meet

In the next visit, Wg Cdr Shukla decided to tell the children more about the shooting competitions that are held and about one of his own exciting experiences. As usual, everyone had gathered in the auditorium and all were eagerly waiting for Shukla. To Shukla's surprise, he found that the size of the audience had visibly increased. He was encouraged and very excited. After due salutations and formalities, he started his talk by saying, "Friends, today I am going to tell you more about how armament firing competitions are conducted. Similar competitions are conducted by almost all the Air Forces of the world. These competitions not only help to improve the marksmanship but also help in generating competitive spirit amongst pilots. They also help in creating some sort of pressure and stress on the pilot, much less, of course, than what the pilot will experience during actual war, but adequate enough to teach him to perform under such trying conditions.

Sqn Ldr Ranjan has already told you that the lowest level at which the competition starts is at the squadron level. All eligible pilots fire rockets, guns and drop bombs on the air-to-ground range and depending on their average scores, the CO selects those pilots who have performed well and forms three teams – one for rockets, second for guns and third for bombing. Likewise, other squadrons also do the same. In addition to these teams, one more team is also selected in air-to-air firing. Air-to-air firing is carried out by firing guns on a banner (target on which guns are fired) which is towed by a target towing aircraft. Those pilots who get good number of hits on the banner are selected in the team.

The next step is to have inter-squadron competition at Command level. I hope you remember that our Air Force is organised in various Commands on geographical basis. We have Western Air Command (WAC), Southwestern Air Command (SWAC), Southern Air Command (SAC), Eastern Air Command (EAC) and Central Air Command (CAC). Besides, we have two functional Commands called Training Command (TC) and Maintenance Command (MC). Each Command barring the functional Commands conduct their own inter-squadron competitions and select the best pilots out of the entire lot to form Command teams.

Once in a year, Air Headquarters (Air HQ) located at Delhi in Vayu Bhavan (VB) conducts Inter-Command competition in which the Command teams take part. Various trophies are then given by the Chief of the Air Staff in a special meeting held at Air HQ to the winners. One trophy goes to the Command which performs the best and bags maximum points. Trophies are also given to the pilots who stand first in the various individual competitions. It's a great and a very thrilling event. Something like, perhaps your inter-house sports tournament conducted in your school or inter-school tournaments.

Let me now narrate to you my own experience in one such competition in which I participated some years back. I still remember that it was January 15 and I was all set to fire the lone rocket as a member of my Command team. I had come up the hard way, starting at squadron level. In the squadron competition, I had fired 20 rockets. Most of my rockets had scored direct hits, meaning bull's eye. Few had gone astray, but since the best 15 rockets were counted for final scoring, I got the best score in the squadron and was, therefore, selected in the squadron team.

In the inter-squadron command meet, I again scored maximum number of direct hits and got a place in the Command team for individual event. And on that day, on January 15, I was mentally preparing myself to fire that one rocket and get a good score for my Command. The tension was mounting. My heart was beating faster. I knew that I had to get a direct hit else my reputation was at stake. I was aware that all other competitors were as good, perhaps better and that I was in a stiff competition. I braced myself and went to the aircraft. The weather was cold but clear and at least one tension of whether I will find the target from the air or not reduced. I inspected the aircraft and the rocket, started up the aircraft and took off. As I took off, surprisingly all the tension melted. The only thought in my mind was how will I aim at the target. It took me ten minutes to reach the range. I contacted the Range Safety Officer (RSO) and requested for his permission to fire that lone rocket. He cleared me and I dived towards the target. I pressed the trigger at what I thought was the right moment and the rocket went. I saw it going and felt that it was heading towards the target. I pulled the aircraft out of the dive and eagerly waited for the RSO to tell me the result. I was exhilirated to hear from him that it was a direct hit. But the jubilation was shortlived. When I landed, everyone praised me but they also told me that one more pilot has achieved a direct hit and, hence, there will be a re-shoot between two of us. So an hour later, I took off again. I think it was my day. I think God was on my side that day because I got a direct hit again, while the other pilot's score was ten yards off the target. Poor chap! — I felt sorry for him because he had also put in as much hard work as I had and come so close to becoming the rocket champion of the year. I suppose it only proved a point that luck is a big factor and fortunately for me it was on my side that day.

There are other instances as well when the tenacity of a fighter pilot is tested. This is done by sending inspection teams to the squadrons. All Air Forces have these inspection branches with a Director General heading that branch. His job is to send a team of qualified members to various squadrons and check their operational efficiency. During their visit, they give contingencies which the squadron is required to tackle. For example, they will simulate a contingency wherein the enemy's Army is rapidly crossing the border with their tanks and they have to be halted, else the war might be lost. Our own Army is doing its best to halt them but they have requested for Air Power to assist them.

Once some such contingency is given, the squadron is then quickly supposed to react to that contingency. It is a race against time. The engineering staff has to quickly get on with the job. The various technicians have to start getting the aircraft ready. The armourers have to get the requisite ammunition from the storage, prepare it for firing and load it on the aircraft. All this has to be accomplished within a laid down time frame.

The pilots have to quickly prepare their strike plan. They have to decide what tactics they will employ to reduce their own attrition meaning prevent their own aircraft from getting shot down by the enemy's AD weapons. Once ready, the strike plan has to be executed. All the activities are closely observed by the various members (known as umpires) of the inspection team. They give marks based on the time taken to complete the various activities. Finally, of course, the scores achieved at the range after firing are taken for evaluation. Based on the final score, the squadron is declared as "operational" meaning fit to participate in war, or declared "non-operational" meaning not fit to fight in the war. Based on the final score, the squadron is also rated as "average", or "below average", or if the squadron has scored very high marks then "Above Average" or even "exceptional". It is a matter of shame for the squadron pilots to be rated as "non-operational" and "below average" because news spreads very quickly in the rest of the Air Force and that squadron is looked down upon and becomes a source of ridicule. The visit of this inspection team causes a lot of tension and all the personnel of the squadron have to perform and perform well under that tension.

Besides these gunnery meets and visits of various inspection teams, there are many other instances which put the fighter pilot under pressure and expect him not to buckle down. One such occasion can be development of some technical fault in the aircraft when one is flying. There are many such emergency situations that can arise and all the pilots are well trained to cope with them. But there can be some situations totally out of the text book for which one may not be prepared. Once I found myself in a very strange situation. I was flying the *Kiran* aircraft. This is the jet trainer manufactured by Hindustan Aeronautics Limited (HAL). Like most fighter jets, it has two main wheels and one nose wheel. They constitute what is called as Undercarriage. When on ground, the aircraft rests on these three wheels and when the aircraft takes off, the undercarriage is retracted, meaning the wheels are withdrawn into the body of the aircraft called fuselage. One day, when I took off, the right main wheel detached itself from the aircraft due to some material failure and I found myself in the air with just two wheels to land on. Had it happened to my car, I would have stopped on the roadside, fitted the spare wheel and carried on without much sweat. But in the air, such a thing was not possible.

Should I land on just two wheels? or should I land on the belly of the aircraft with the two wheels retracted? or should I eject? — I had to decide. Chances of fire due to friction during belly landing were high. Whereas the chances of right wing touching the runway because of no wheel being on the right side and then the aircraft going out of control also weighed on my mind. This emergency situation was completely out of any textbook. I decided to land on two wheels and informed the ATC accordingly. He alerted the Crash Tender and ambulance and got them ready if the aircraft go out of control. As I came on final approach and was about to land, everyone was tensed up and so was

I but I managed to keep the right wing up for a while, lowered it gently and kept the aircraft straight using left brake. It was indeed a strange emergency situation I had to cope with but fortunately it got well handled and a major disaster was averted."

Wg Cdr Shukla finally wound up his interesting talk saying, "Hope you enjoyed listening to what I told you today. Next time, I will bring with me a friend who will narrate to you a very interesting experience which he had during one war game which was held last year. The prime function of all Air Forces, in fact, all Armed Forces, is to be ever ready to fight a war. To ensure that, war games are organised in which various contingencies are simulated and the forces are tested for their war preparedness. Next talk will be on the conduct of one such war game. Bye, till then."

12 ▸ War Gaming

A month later, Wg Cdr Paranjape arrived in the school, on invitation from the Principal. Wg Cdr Shukla had already briefed him about what to tell and about what all has been already told to the children, so that he does not repeat any subject. Wg Cdr Paranjape started his talk after paying respects to the Principal and other staff members saying, "Good morning friends, Wg Cdr Shukla has conveyed his regrets for not being able to come today, since he has to fly on an important mission. Nevertheless, he has told me about how keen and interested you all are to hear about the classical way in which war games are conducted by the various Armed Forces of the world."

Let me begin by telling you a famous statement made by one of the Generals. He said, "Most people think that Armed Forces are created at a huge cost to fight and win a war. Well, that is not entirely so. The main aim behind arming our Armed Forces by spending huge sums of money is to deter the enemy from attacking us and should that deterrence fail, then the Armed Forces should be able to defeat the enemy in a short swift war. Armed Forces are thus more for avoiding a war rather than fighting a war because war is a very expensive proposition and can economically put a country back more than ten years".

The last full-scale war which our defence forces actually fought and won was in 1971 against Pakistan. Thereafter, we haven't fought a full-scale war in its true sense. There have been indeed some limited wars like in Kargil or in Sri Lanka where we sent our troops or in Congo but these skirmishes have given very limited exposure to just few of our troops. Almost all the personnel who fought the 71 War have now retired and today, we have a bunch of soldiers, pilots and other officers in the three Services who have no experience of participating in a war. So, how to overcome this deficiency? Well, the best answer in today's high-tech scenario is to conduct computer aided war games.

Almost all the countries have war colleges which conduct regular courses to teach the art and science of war fighting to their personnel. We, in India, also have war colleges run by the three Services. After being taught the theory, covering the strategy and tactics of war fighting, the students are tested in the application of this theory by making them participate in war games.

All the students of the three war colleges assemble in one selected college and for nearly one month participate in the combined war game. The students are divided into two groups – one group is generally called the Blue Land Forces and the other Red Land Forces. The Commanders-in-Chief for the two forces are nominated so also the Commanders at various levels of war fighting. The two sides are allocated with forces in terms of soldiers, tanks, artillery, fighter aircraft, transport aircraft, helicopters, ships, frigates, carrier, etc. A fictitious scenario is painted for them . For example, they could be told that the Red Land is very poor in natural resources and fears that it may run out of energy in terms of oil since many sanctions have been imposed on them by the leading World Powers. The Dictator ruling the Red Land is rather rebellious and has stepped up his defiance ever since he has obtained nuclear weapons. On the other side, Blue Land, also a nuclear power, is a democracy rich in oil reserves and more prosperous. They have few oil wells very close to the Red Land border and it is feared that Red Land may attack them to gain control over these oil wells.

Having painted such picture to both sides in much more details than what I have just told you, the two sides are then separated into different rooms. Commanders of the two sides are given about 7 to 10 days to do their appreciation of the situation, plan the deployment of their forces and also make offensive and defensive plans. Thereafter, the Control Room occupied by the staff members of the three colleges calls the two sides one by one and asks them to present their plans. The plans are thoroughly scrutinised by asking the reason and logic behind each deployment and the actions narrated in the plans. Based on how the plans of both the sides mesh, one side is told to execute its plans.

In this case, let us say that Blue Land is given the initiative, considering that their stated aim and objective is to first neutralise the nuclear capability of Red Land. Incidentally, all the deployment of forces of both the sides is entered in the master computer of the Control room and so also the strike plans of both sides. If the preemptive strike planned by Blue Land Commander is to attack Red Land airfields, communication centres and nuclear capability-related-vital points with a large number of their strike aircraft, then this plan is played in the computer against the air defence plan given by the Red Land Force Commander.

The computer has pre-fed data related to the performance of various weapons and other equipments like radars, tanks, aircraft, etc. The computer decides on the success or failure of various strike missions that are executed and produces a comprehensive result sheet giving the number of aircraft shot down from both sides, when and in what situation. The result sheet also gives the damage caused to the attacked targets. Based on this, the control team informs the two sides about the damage sustained by both the sides and asks them to immediately react to this situation. The Red Land then reacts and launches a counter offensive. This is then played on the computer and various different contingencies are generated and Commanders on both the sides are immediately required to react. The process is continued and at an appropriate time, the game is stopped.

At the end of the game, both sides are called and a very detailed debrief and discussion is held which lasts for days. Many questions starting with "Why?", "Why not?" "What if?" are asked and important lessons learnt. The beauty of computer war gaming is that no actual damage is caused to the equipment used and yet lessons are learnt. Mock war games with actual deployment of forces is also held to give practice to warriors of the three Services to get actual experience in moving and deploying their equipment. This is also important because it gives the warriors hands on experience in using their equipment. I have been fortunate to have got lot of chances to participate in many war games and also in conducting war games when I was posted as Chief Instructor (War Gaming) in the College of Air Warfare. There is just one important thing that I want to tell you. A computer must be used as an aid for planning and not as a device to do the planning for you. Many feel that a computer can do excellent planning but they must remember that computer planning will be only as good as the data and various algorithms fed into it and the data may not always be up-to-date and correct. Besides that, the human element which is a very important factor in war fighting, is not factored in computer planning. The Commander, therefore, must take help of the computer but take his own decisions to factor in surprise and his expertise built over the years through training and experience. Thank you all very much. It was nice talking to such an involved audience. Hope you all enjoyed the talk."

All the students gave him a standing applause. The Principal too thanked Wg Cdr Paranjape for having spared his time to visit the school and interact with the children. He further requested him to inform Wg Cdr Shukla that students were very keen to know about how fighter aircraft fly at night, specially in dark night, when there is no moon light and when it is totally dark and difficult to even walk in pitch darkness. Wg Cdr Paranjape promised to convey his request to Wg Cdr Shukla who he mentioned would definitely visit the school to tell them about night flying and if possible take the interested students to the Air Force Station to witness night flying.

13 ▸ Night Flying

Fifteen days went by and the phase of the moon changed. It was a new moon (no moon) night. This implied that the night would be pitch dark with no moonlight whatsoever. Wg Cdr Shulka decided to visit the school and invite the interested students to the Air Force station to witness how aircraft fly in pitch dark night. Shulka took the Principal's permission to visit the school which the Principal gave readily. He felt happy to see a lot of interested students waiting for him eagerly.

Shukla began his talk, saying, "Friends, today I have brought along with me Wg Cdr Dhillon who will tell you about his hair raising experience when he was flying at night in dark phase. But before I hand over to Dhillon, let me tell you in brief about the various phases of the moon. This is important for pilots to know. The 28 days cycle of the moon is divided into two phases. One is called the "dark phase" and the other as "moon phase". Moon phase starts a week after the no moon or new moon night and continues till a week after Full moon.

The moon is entirely invisible when the moon comes in between the earth and the sun (no moon or new moon night). When the earth comes in between the sun and the moon, the moon appears "full" as a bright round disc (full moon night). Starting from the new moon, the moon's illuminated surface appears to grow slowly to half to full moon and then decreases to half and then to the next new moon. The moonlight, consequently, also increases slowly from new moon to full moon and then slowly decreases from full moon to the new moon.

The phases of the moon are caused by the relative positions of the earth, sun and the moon as the moon orbits the earth. The first and third quarter moons, also called as half moons, happen when the moon is at a 90 degrees angle with respect to the earth and the sun. So we see exactly half of the moon illuminated and half in shadow.

The position of moonrise and moonset like that of sun rise and sunset varies as the earth goes around the sun and also with the phases of the moon. During the new moon phase, the moonrise and moonset is along with the sunrise and sunset. In the first quarter, when the moon is half visible, it rises at local noon and sets at local midnight. On full moon day, the moonrise is at sun set and the moonset is at sunrise. In the third quarter, the moon rises at local midnight and sets at local noon.

When a pilot commences to learn night flying, he is first taught to fly during the moon phase which lasts for 14 days from half moon to full moon to half moon. Having gathered adequate experience in flying during moon phase, he then graduates to dark phase flying. I will now hand over to Wg Cdr Dhillon who will narrate to you his experience during one of his sorties in dark phase."

Wg Cdr Dhillon wished everyone a wonderful morning and commenced his talk, "Well friends, let me first tell you what all is involved in the conduct of night flying. Night flying also starts with the Met Briefing exactly the way it is conducted before commencing day flying. The Met officer first gives the actual and the expected weather brief in and around the airfield. Then the ATC Officer briefs about the state of the runway which is called as flare path about which I will tell you more in details shortly. He also briefs about the serviceability of various flying aids like GCA, ILS, AD 210, etc about which you all have already been told. The DATCO also briefs on the watch hours of various radars. The Engineering Officer then briefs about the availability and serviceability of various fighter aircraft.

This Met Briefing is followed by what is called as the emergency session. In this session, an emergency is given at random to any of the pilots who have been programmed to fly that night. The emergency could cover a system failure in the aircraft or a situation like sudden appearance of low clouds or rain or blockage of runway due to tyre burst while landing or some such contingency. The idea behind this emergency session is to revise and freshen up the correct actions that need to be taken in any such contingencies.

Let me now show you the picture of a flare path. Notice the yellow lead-in lights. The beginning of the flare path is marked by blue lights.

Since the runway cannot be seen at night the way it can be seen during day time, it needs to be lit with what are called as runway lights. The runway lighting system consists of lights placed on either edge of the runway at fixed distances. Lights are also placed at the beginning of the runway, at its middle to indicate the half way point and at the end in a particular pattern which all pilots are aware of. The electrical supply to this entire system is drawn from the commercial grid. But if this commercial supply suddenly fail and the lights go off, then it can result in an accident if a pilot is about to land. To cater for this eventuality, there is a backup supply which is provided by the standby generator system which resumes the electrical supply automatically within a few seconds and the lights come on almost immediately.

Night flying is actually very safe. In fact, contrary to what most people feel, it is safer than day flying. You may be surprised to know that the accident rate during night flying in almost all the Air Forces of the world is much lower than during day flying. Now, I will narrate to you a strange experience which I had during one of the dark night sorties which I flew few months back.

It was the month of July when the monsoon was quite active. The night was pitch dark. I had to fly a sortie at almost midnight. I reached the squadron at seven in the evening which was the scheduled time for night flying briefing. The Met Officer had predicted a cloudy night but no rain. The sun had just set. It was dusk period and sunlight was slowly dissipating. The orange shaded sky with patches of clouds was looking beautiful and inviting.

I was planned to fly a PI (Practice Interception) sortie in a fighter aircraft as interceptor along with another pilot in another fighter who was to act as target aircraft. I started up my aircraft at 2330h for a scheduled take-off at 2345h. Having carried out all my checks and vital actions prior to take-off, I asked ATC for permission to enter the flare path for take-off. The pilot who was supposed to act as target aircraft for me had already taken off. My take-off was normal and I enjoyed it. I commenced my climb to 15,000 ft to carry out a look up interception and missile attack on the target which was at 20,000 ft.

I think, I should tell you about various types of interceptions in brief. Interception basically means to steer a particular course given by the Fighter Controller (FC) which will make you meet the target. Basically there are three types of interceptions. One is called the head-on interception in which you approach the target in more or less in opposite direction. The other is tail-on in which you approach the target from his rear quarters and the third is beam interception in which the target is approached from an angle of 90 degrees to its flight path. The approach can be either from same level as the target or from bottom-up (also called look-up) which means from below the target height or top-down (also called look-down) which means from a height above the target height. Which type of interception to adopt is decided by the Fighter Controller depending upon the relative position of the target aircraft with respect to the attacker aircraft as seen by him on the ground radar scope.

That night, I was supposed to practice a look-up beam interception. Having climbed to 15,000 ft, I contacted the Fighter Controller (FC) who gave me directions to steer my aircraft. The night was pitch dark and I could see only a few lights on the ground. The presence of clouds was very disturbing. I could not see the horizon and it was getting difficult to stay oriented and yet I smartly follow the Fighter Controller's instructions. I had to stay glued to my flying instruments in the cockpit and concentrate very hard to stay right side up. Artificial Horizon about which you have been told was the main instrument which was helping me to stay upright. Though I was concentrating very hard, I started getting a feeling that I was upside down. The artificial horizon and other instruments contradicted this feeling but still the feeling of being upside down was so strong that it would not go. I realised that I was experiencing disorientation — a cause for many accidents. My past experience and training came to my aid. I decided to disregard my feelings and believe what the instruments were telling me and that saved me.

Disorientation is a state wherein one is unable to recognise where one is or where one should go or a state in which one is terribly confused. The moment one cannot perceive where one is in relation to the horizon, time, place or space that state can be called as a condition of disorientation. Generally, this phenomenon does not affect a pilot while flying during daytime on clear visibility days and that is because the sense of sight acts supreme and overrules the perceptions of the other senses. Even if one does a violent combat manoeuvre, as long as one can clearly see the horizon, one will remain oriented. But the moment one loses visual contact with the horizon, things can be quite different.

The main cause of disorientation is the vestibular canal located in the ear. The vestibular apparatus consists of three semi-circular canals at right angles to each other and the hair cells floating in the fluids in these canals. These tiny hair cells send information to the brain about the position and orientation of the person. When these hair are disturbed due to some violent motion of the head, they send wrong signals and that results in a feeling of disorientation. Just as an experiment, I want you all to close your eyes and shake your head vigorously up, down and sideways and then with eyes closed try and stand up. I am sure that most of you will feel imbalanced on your feet. But the moment you open your eyes, you will regain your balance because vision is the most dominant sensor in deciding the orientation. Anyone of you ever got slapped hard on the ear? I am sure those of you who did must have lost balance and wondered for a while as to where you are.

I am reminded of the disorientation which I had experienced when flying in a pitch dark night over the sea. Though I was quite alert and scanning all the instruments meticulously, I experienced a feeling as if I am tilted to the left – not just a bit but quite a lot. The

Artificial Horizon didn't indicate so. I made the mistake of looking out to stabilise myself by seeing the horizon but since there was no visible horizon, the movement of the head and, consequently, of the hair cells of the ear made me even more confused. I had to really fight this feeling and trust my instruments. I gingerly turned towards the airbase and when I saw the town lights, my senses suddenly got stabilised. It was a crazy experience, which no doubt, had scared me a lot.

There are many other kinds of disorientation. There is a funny kind of disorientation which even some of you might have experienced. It is really crazy, how at times one starts imagining and seeing things when they actually don't exist, but one desperately wants to see them – this is also a kind of disorientation. For example, if one is looking for one's mother or wife in a crowded place like a mall, then every lady whom you see looks as if she is your mother or wife and one gets confused. Sometimes when one goes on visits and sleeps elsewhere and happens to get up in the middle of night one wonders for a while as to where one is and takes a little time getting stabilised. This too is some sort of crazy disorientation.

Disorientation is indeed a strange phenomenon. Best is to be pre-warned and pre-armed against it. Learn to detect it early and fight it. One will be more prone to it if one is flying in dark night with no external reference or in clouds or on a mucky day. One should not fly with a cold or when not fully fit or when fatigued. The most important mantra when experiencing disorientation is to trust the flying instruments. The modern instruments are more reliable sensors than one's vestibular apparatus.

Well, thank you very much for listening to me so patiently and with such interest. I really enjoyed talking to you all. Now, may I invite those of you who are interested in watching the night flying that is going to take place in the Air Force station at 1900h sharp. We will take you on top of the ATC from where you will get an excellent view of all take-offs and landings." The students were overjoyed on hearing the invitation and whole lot of them promised to visit the station.

14 ▸ The Dare Devils

Air Force Day was approaching and planning for the celebrations had started in earnest in all the Air Force stations. As a part of celebrations, the IAF aerobatic team was scheduled to visit various major towns and conduct displays to increase awareness in general population about the Air Force. The team was planned to arrive and perform sometimes in the second half of September in the town where Vikram resided. When Wg Cdr Shukla came to know of this, he felt that calling the school children to witness the show of the IAF team would act as a great incentive for them to join this exciting profession. He, therefore, rang up the Principal and requested him for a visit to the school to educate the children about formation aerobatics and to invite them to the Air Force station to witness the display of the aerobatic team. The Principal accepted his request with great enthusiasm. A day before the aerobatics team was to arrive, Wg Cdr Shukla visited the school.

He commenced his talk like this: "Friends, today I am going to tell you about those pilots of the IAF whom I would like to call as the "dare devils" because of their bravery and exceptional flying skill. I am talking about those pilots who form the IAF aerobatic team. But first, let me give you a brief history about formation flying in the Air Force.

Some of you may be aware that the Indian Air Force was formed on October 8, 1932. As such, the Air Force Day is celebrated every year with great pride and dignity. The main celebration is held in Delhi. Earlier the celebrations were held at Palam airbase. The display included an impressive parade done by the air warriors followed by a magnificent flypast with almost all the aircraft in the inventory of IAF and an outstanding formation aerobatic display put up by the IAF aerobatic team called "Suryakirans". A few years back, the helicopters too joined in and put up a marvelous display equipped with HAL built ALH. Since the civil airlines traffic was getting affected adversely, the celebrations have been shifted to an IAF airbase called Hindon located close to Delhi. Formation Flying Displays have also been a great source of attraction for the general public during Republic Day celebrations.

Formation Aerobatics has been a part of the Indian Air Force aviation history for a very long time. The history would go back to even before 1964, when four Mysteres flew past in a "Box" formation over Delhi on Republic Day. During the golden jubilee year of the IAF in 1982, hand picked fighter pilots from various squadrons formed an aerobatic team for the IAF called "The Thunderbolts". This nine Hunter aircraft Team enjoyed a glorious innings for nearly a decade. The Hunter aircraft were painted deep blue with streaks of lightning passing all through. They performed throughout the country giving immense joy to the common man who watched them in great awe. The Thunderbolts gave their last public display in 1989.

In 1990, the Hunters were phased out and the indigenously manufactured Kiran MK II aircraft were selected to form the IAF aerobatic team. Initially, the team started as a four aircraft team. In early 1996, serious planning began for Aero India-96, the first major air show and aviation trade event ever hosted in India. To put up a grand show, the organisers wanted to invite an aerobatic team from overseas. However, senior IAF officers were confident that the IAF would be able to field its own team. Thus, the Suryakiran team was formed in 1996 as a 6-aircraft team. By 1997, the team had been expanded to 9 aircraft.

The Suryakiran Team exploits the potential of the Kiran Mk II aircraft to its limits. Formation flying with two aircraft is comparatively an easy task on this machine. Nine aircraft Formation Aerobatics, however, is an altogether different matter. Maintaining correct position requires excellent reflexes, anticipation and a lot of determination. Those are the qualities that bind the team together to produce the orchestrated manoeuvres which the audience witnesses.

The nine aircraft take off in VICs of three, one behind the other in close succession and join up in close formation. The formation performs various manoeuvres between speeds of 150 and 650 Kmph. During the manoeuvres, the distance between the aircraft is as less as 5 metres. The various profiles undertaken are a series of dynamic combinations resulting in constantly changing formations. This subjects the pilots to alternating 'g' forces between +6 to –1.5. Perfection comes only with practice and that is the reason why the team looks at each and every manoeuvre in detail on the ground. It is then flown and finally debriefed with the help of video recordings. Thus, emerges the 15-20 minutes of aerial choreography of the pilots.

The team has performed all over India in practically all the major towns and successfully enthralled the crowds. They have even performed in foreign countries like Sri Lanka and Singapore. So, if you want to feel absolutely elated, you have to personally see the team performing from close quarters. They even got an opportunity to perform along with the RAF team called "Red Arrows" when they were passing through Delhi on their way to Singapore. The Red Arrows perform their aerobatics on the Hawk aircraft which we have recently acquired for advanced training of our fighter pilots. Some of our Suryakiran pilots got a chance to sit in the Hawk during their display performance and learn from them. Similarly, when the

French Aerobatic Team passed through Air Force station, Pune, the Suryakirans also put up a matching display along with them. Those who saw both these displays felt very proud to note that the Suryakiran display was as good. Some Suryakiran pilots also flew in the Alpha Jet which the French Aerobatic Team called *Patrouille Acrobatique de France* uses for their display.

Now, I will show you some of the photographs taken during the performance put up by the Suryakirans. First have a close look at the Kiran Mk II aircraft in raw colour which the team flies.

HAL Built Kiran Jet Trainer Aircraft

Now, watch some fascinating photographs taken during the performance. I am sure you will get motivated enough to come and see the display which is planned tomorrow. Don't be late. You must watch them right from take-off till they land and I am sure you will enjoy thoroughly.

In an immaculate formation flying the tri-colour

On the back of the loop

In a classic burst to reform again

Crossing dangerously close

I hope you all enjoyed watching these few fabulous photographs. Well, those of you who want to enjoy seeing the Suryakirans perform live are cordially invited to the Air Force station not later than 0700hrs. The entry gates will be closed exactly at 0700h because the show is expected to commence soon thereafter. And please don't bring any eatables because they attract birds which can be dangerous specially during this performance when so many aircraft are huddled up so close. Thank you and see you tomorrow."

Vikram, his close friend Inder and many other students along with the school staff and the Pricipal reached the Air Force station promptly a few minutes before 0700h. They were received by Wg Cdr Shukla and taken up to the balcony adjoining the ATC from where they got an excellent view of the display. They all were spellbound. Later, they were taken to the Kiran aircraft and given a chance to sit in the cockpit and also meet the daring pilots of the aerobatic team. That was the day Vikram and Inder decided to become fighter pilots and DARE TO ENJOY.

❋ ❋ ❋